THE ANTICHRISTMAS PRESENT

Horror Stories

Kevin Sweeney

Black Rainbows Press

For the Godless

A special thank you goes to the following people; Simon McHardy, Gerhard Jason Geick, Nikolas P. Robinson, Rayne Havok, Dani Brown, the Mothers of Mayhem Christina Pfeiffer and Marian Echevarria...

And, of course, Drew Stepek.

CONTENTS

THE MUST HAVE

"I WANT it, please, I want it, please get it for me! I'll die if I don't get it!" whined Jordan.

Mort frowned.

"You said that about the..."

Jordan crossed his arms.

"I know what I said, but I was wrong," he patiently told his father. "I want this one. You promised!"

It was their Xmas tradition. Mort took his son to a bricks-and-mortar toy shop to pick the present he wanted to find under the tree.

He took the box from the shelf.

Weird. It was the only one on display. Maybe it was really popular, and this was the only one left?

It was in a cardboard carton with a clear plastic window allowing the contents to be viewed. These contents were secured in place by twists of plastic, and included not only the doll, but a number of accessories.

It was supposed to be some sort of a clown, fuzzy neon hair, big red nose. Giant head on a small body, wide staring eyes that seemed to follow you, maniacal grin that was less cheerful than a skull's grimace. It wore a sort of white smock decorated with red polka dots, if polka dots were what the irregular crimson stains were supposed to be…

And the accessories...was that a miniature chainsaw?

"Why don't we keep looking," said Mort. He managed to keep any trace of the unease he felt out of his voice. It was only a fucking doll, for god's sake... "I'm sure you'll find something else you want just as bad, and you'll forgot all about..." he read the funfair writing on the box, "*Splatters the Clown*. Ugh."

It may have been that "ugh" that sealed the deal.

"No dad, I want this one," said Jordan. "I've made up my mind. You said I could have one toy from this place, and this is what I'm picking."

Mort wondered if he could attach a string or two this late in the negotiations.

He looked for a price for the thing, but there was none on the box, and none on any of the little plastic plaques on the shelf. The prices on similar toys on either side of the lonely space Splatters had been were well within his budget, so if the unnerving little clown was of a kind to its neighbours, he couldn't cry off due to expense.

He looked at the doll again.

A clown.

Was its grin… wider?

Were its eyes… shinier?

"Dad, you promised..."

He had, yes.

Bollocks.

He bought the toy.

*****

It killed them all.

Of course it fucking did.

Jordan choked on one of the toy's accessories, within hours of getting it out of the box on Xmas morning.

His mum was unable to process the grief at the loss of her son, and less than a week after his small, sad little funeral stepped in front of a train.

And Mort, delirious with guilt, drank himself to death.

ORIGIN STORY

IT WAS no surprise for him to be condemned to Hell when he died. He knew what he was in life, and that damnation awaited him after. This was why he had indulged himself so mightily, why there were so many bodies. His appetite would pass into legend, a man who had stolen away such vast quantities of the innocent that a folk tale would need to be wrapped around the horror of what he had done, a tale that the little ones had been eaten by a swarm of rats, not a man in pied motley who had tempted them away, and as the years would pass the story would become warped, would change...

So many children stolen, fucked, and partially devoured. His clothes had been pied, yes, but became soaked in blood they were crimson forever after.

Hell could hold no worse than him.

There was no punishment that could ever equal his crimes.

He was wrong.

The infernal powers conceived of the worst of all torments for him. For one night out of every year they allowed him free reign upon the Earth, to go where he would invisibly, to venture into the bed chambers of innocents as he had in life... but he could not tempt them with the gifts he brought, for no matter how much his loins and his teeth ached for their flesh, he could not touch them.

The agony of that single night tormented him for an entire year, would gnaw at him as he wished to gnaw their bones, would pierce his soul as he wished to plunder their bodies... and as hours and days passed the unsatisfied ravening lessened until it seemed he could bear his burden, a year would have passed and once more he would make his vigil over every sleeping child across the Earth.

And to grind salt into the open wounds of his soul, the final insult for being at the top of the naughty list... they'd traded his pipe for jingling bells.

JUST WHAT SHE WANTED

AS JULES festooned the tree she fumed, but with every new addition to the green and spiky boughs her anger very slowly began to ebb… which was ironic, because it was the fact that Den hadn't even bothered to get the decorations out of the attic that had caused her to finally boil over and…

She closed her eyes, breathed deeply.

No, she had had her explosion, she wasn't going to blow her lid again. There was still too much to get done.

One thing at a time.

Now, the tree.

The smell of sap and pine needles was calming. It almost covered the smell of blood.

So much to do; the shopping, for example. Between them they had two sets of parents, a brother, a sister, and a brother-in-law, plus two nieces and a nephew. There were ten presents to be accounted for right there, not even including gifts for each of them –because, of course, she would have to buy her gift to herself from Den, because he was so utterly hopeless- and even if she bought all the gifts on-line, she still had to find the time to sit down with her tablet and put the thought and effort into trying to get everyone things they might actually want... but at least her sister's kids had emailed an extensive list of things they expected.

Jules held up something round and glistening that wasn't a bauble in the traditional sense. She pierced it with a fishing hook and hung it on the tree. It squirted slime onto her fingers when the metal pierced its thick membrane, slime that she had on a few occasions in the past, such as birthdays, swallowed.

And that was just the shopping for presents. Shopping for food was a whole different matter... particularly because it was there year to have Den's parents over, and his gormless work-shy brother who still lived with them. It wasn't just the food for the big day –reserving a turkey at Waitrose, gluten-free stuffing, Brussel sprouts and potatoes and carrots and parsnips that would all have to be washed and peeled and chopped and timed so that everything came out together ready for the table where Den would make a holy show of dismembering the bird with an electric meat carver- but laying in enough supplies to keep everyone full of festive fucking cheer until New Year's...

Den couldn't be trusted to go down the chip shop and come back with cod and pea fritters twice, let alone turkey and trimmings –*chipolatas, must remember chipolatas for the pigs in blankets!*- and all the booze that would be needed to ensure everyone was just drunk enough to pretend they were enjoying themselves.

Jules wound a length of something purple and slippery around the tree like it was the tinsel that was still in the attic. If she squeezed it too hard, partially digested Coronation chicken baguette mixed with cappuccino and Snickers oozed out of the torn end.

The house had to be cleaned ready for the descent of seasonal well-wishers who would expect to be fed and watered. Presents had to be wrapped for her sister's snot-nosed little shits. Cards had to be written to people they hadn't seen in a half dozen years.

And then, after it was all over, there was the little matter of paying for the season… which would require Jules to start looking for a second job because Den couldn't possibly put in any more hours at the warehouse sitting on his fucking arse in the office.

Red dripped from the tree. Red and green; very festive.

Jules had asked Den to do one thing; get a tree and decorate it.

He had gotten the tree.

And then pointed out that buying a tree and then decorating it were, in fact, two jobs, and he had already put in a full week, he needed some time for himself, it wasn't like she was rushed off her feet when you could get all the shopping delivered, and what was the point of sending cards anymore, wouldn't a phone call be more personal, more eco-friendly…

Jules wasn't a sociopath. She had had a miscarriage two weeks previously which she had not told Den about because he hadn't known she was pregnant. It was going to be her present to him on the big day, the news. So when she snapped it wasn't just because she was stressed over things like parsnips and pigs in blankets.

Not entirely, anyway.

Jules had just located the electric carving knife in its place at the back of the cupboard when her husband had suggested that this whole Christmas lark was "a doddle nowadays, not like when my mum was doing the honours when I was a kid…"

She needed a footstool to reach the top of the tree. The fairy, like the lights and the baubles and the tinsel, was still soundly tucked away in one of a half dozen shoe boxes in the attic, so in her place Jules piked her husband's head. The skin around his neck was ragged from being carved through by twin serrated blades whizzing back and forth, and his expression was the same look of astonishment he had worn when she had plunged the buzzing knife into his chest.

His mouth was open. You could see the spiky brown top-branches bunched in the back of his throat.

Jules smiled, and raised a blood smeared glass of something fizzy.

She hadn't asked him for much.

She had just wanted him to decorate the tree.

THE OTHER 364 DAYS OF THE YEAR

SHE WAS the smallest whore ever.

She was perfect.

Letwin pulled over to the curb.

Was she a child?

No, when she turned to look at him it was obvious that she wasn't; she was the size of a child, yes, but her face was old.

He could work with that though.

His window was down, but she could barely see over it, so he had to lean part of the way out.

"You want some company?" she asked.

Her voice made him pause. It had a weird lilt, sort of sing-song, as if she was about to break into rhyme like a fairy tale character.

Most whores sounded hard and joyless.

And her eyes…

But she was dressed in the uniform of the professional sex-worker –dyed hair, cheap, short skirt ready to be dropped at a nod, tits almost hanging out, high heels and too much make-up- so Letwin asked her to get in, he had a proposal.

She must have been new to the scene, because she was fucking stupid enough to agree to it.

*****

Letwin did not think of himself as a bad bloke. If, he reasoned, he had been a bad bloke, he wouldn't have picked up the odd prostitute from time to time to indulge in his fantasy.

The fantasy was his release. It was what stopped him from being a monster.

He did not go to certain websites.

He did not use encryption software to discretely buy pictures and videos.

He did not hang around schools or playgrounds, and he had never flown to certain countries where very little money could purchase anything you wanted.

He knew what he was, and he fought against it. When you got right down to it, he was a hero.

The fantasy was like purging.

As long as he could take a prozzy somewhere quiet from time to time, and pretend she was five years old for an hour... or however long they survived.

*****

"You don't live here," said Carol in her voice which wasn't a typical whore's voice.

Her... twinkly voice.

Twinkly. That was the word for it.

The limited small talk in the car had turned over that her name was Carol.

"Yeah, sure, this is my place," he told her.

It wasn't, but how the fuck did she know?

Not that it mattered much. She was already inside, and no-one had seen them come in together.

Letwin had put down a deposit on a six month lease of the dingy little single-bedroom flat, even though he only needed it for this one night. He'd paid cash.

"No," she told him, looking around at the sparsely furnished space, sagging sofa, stained carpet tiles, the lack of pictures on the wall. "You don't live here. No-one does."

He had taken off his coat and was in the tiny foot space that laughingly served as a kitchen, making them drinks.

"What makes you say that?" he asked, warily.

She shrugged.

"We have a good sense for where everyone is in this world," she said.

He looked up from pouring.

That was a fucking weird thing to say.

"Eh?" he said.

She was stood there with her arms folded, looking at him.

Her eyes were…was she wearing contact lenses? Letwin could swear her pupils were misshapen.

"Are you a dwarf?" he asked.

She tilted her head.

Kevin Sweeney

"I mean, your medical condition," he said. "You being so fucking small. No, wait, dwarfs have oversized heads don't they? You're a midget."

"I'm an elf," she said.

Letwin considered this.

"Is that the politically correct word for it? Load of bollocks, all that woke shit."

He held out a glass for her.

She took it from him.

"I mean I'm an elf," she told him. She took a sip and made a face. "What is this?"

"VodKA and coke."

She handed it back to him.

"I like the coke. Could I just have that?"

Letwin widened his eyes. A whore that didn't drink? He downed hers and filled the glass again with Tesco's own brand cola.

This time she drank half of it straight down.

"Could I have some sugar in this?"

"You want sugar in it? That's full fat!"

"I have a very sweet tooth," she told him.

Letwin gazed at her.

"Because you're an elf, right?" he asked her.

She shrugged.

He actually did have sugar amongst his few supplies, and he poured it straight from the bag into the glass, which fizzed up.

She thanked him and drank the lot.

"You're an elf prostitute," said Letwin, sort of like a question.

"I'm an elf," she said. "And I'm selling my body. So, yeah. We doing this or what?"

"An elf? Seriously? Like the magic fairy sort of creature?"

Letwin goggled at her, and then he laughed.

"Fuck me! You're an elf, like the kind who works for Santa, yeah?"

He laughed more.

"You're having a fucking bubble, right?"

Carol said nothing.

"Okay, alright," he said. "So tell me, how does an elf end up whoring then?"

At first he thought she wasn't going to answer. Then she did.

"Christmas is only one day a year. What do you think we do for the other 364?"

Letwin had no idea what to say to that.

"So," said Carol. "We agreed on five hundred for what you want?"

That was standard; just about every whore he had ever made his proposal to had called him every filthy name under the sun... but had acquiesced when the remuneration he suggested got to that magic number.

Carol hadn't called him anything at all.

He still offered her the five hundred however, because he had no intention of paying her.

"Is the bedroom through there?"

Letwin downed his drink.

"It certainly is," he told her. "And from this point on, call me daddy."

*****

The claw hammer was hidden under the inflatable camping mattress. In previous encounters in other rented flats he had kept it closer to hand, under the pillow, but then a young lady of the night called Chemise had found it, had some questions about why it was there, and things had gotten messy long before he had wanted them too.

Under the mattress was still close enough to fetch it at the magic moment.

Carol was naked and lying on her back on the thin sheets of the mattress on the floor.

She had no tits and almost no pubes.

Her cunt was just a split in smooth skin, a split that was a triangle shape, tapering to a point below a small patch of precisely shaved hair.

She was better than perfect.

Letwin was so hard it fucking hurt.

He crept up on her, a beast, a monster, huge and rampant and ready to destroy.

He snuffled between her legs.

Up close, the tiny patch of shaved pubic hair was the shape of a star.

With the tapering triangle of her vagina beneath it, it looked a bit like…

He reeled back.

A Christmas tree; triangular body, tiny star atop it.

Letwin frowned.

Then Carol called him "daddy" and he was the beast again and suddenly he was on top of her, inside her, and oh holy fucking shit it felt amazing, it felt like he had always imagined it would; he was absolutely fucking enormous, stretching her out, stuffing her so full he was slamming into her cervix before he'd even crammed half his inches into her tiny, tight cunt.

She cried out in pain, and that just drove him insane.

Her whole body was sliding up and down the sheets, he was practically able to lift her off the mattress with just his cock, and he had to grip her child-like waist in both hands to pull her onto him as he thrust harder and harder.

He felt something split.

Carol screamed.

He backhanded her to shut her up.

Looking down, he could see the shape of his cock just beneath the flesh of her stomach, a vast maggot eating into her guts.

He was so close…

He pressed one hand against her flat chest whilst his other reached for the edge of the mattress and the hammer concealed beneath.

Letwin's fingers found the rubber grip of the tool and he tugged it lose as he continued to drive her body down into the mattress, relishing the tears that she was shedding, barely hearing her pleas for him to stop, please, as he clawed at the arm that was restraining her…

Then the hammer was up, high in the air above them.

He was holding it the wrong way around, so that at the moment he came and brought it down on her face it was the clawed side of the head that punched through her right cheek, just below her eye.

Letwin was barely aware of it as he came, wrenching it free and ripping a portion of her face off.

He brought it down again, on her mouth, and smashed all her front teeth, upper and lower, back down her throat.

And again, and again, and again; the hammer rose and fell as he rode the rollercoaster of the longest, fiercest orgasm he had ever had, smashing her features back into her head, turning her face into a crater of burst muscle and ripped skin and crazy jags of bone, blood flying from the hammer head in sprays across the pillow and the wall behind it.

Finally, the last glorious spasms went twitching up the length of his deflating cock and into the base of his spine, and he dropped the hammer beside the bed and knelt there between her legs, panting.

"Fuck," he gasped. "Fuck! Oh, fuck!"

He looked down at Carol.

Her eyes had survived the assault, but had come unmoored from the sockets that had been smashed, so that they were in the very centre of the red pit of her buckled in skull, shattered teeth framing them.

Her dyed blonde hair was fanned out like sun beams to show her ears.

Ears that were pointed.

And those eyes…

Her pupils.

Her pupils were the shape of snowflakes, in irises the colour of polished silver.

*****

The clean-up was a lot quicker than usual. Because she was so small, Letwin decided he didn't need to cut her up. He simply bent Carol's body in two, sitting her up and then forward onto her own legs, and stamped on her back until he felt her spine snap and he could fold her in two.

He bundled her up in the sheet, and quietly smiled to himself when he realised that what he had created looked like a big, fucked up present... or possibly a toy sack, which he hefted onto his back and quietly took out to his car.

Ho, ho, ho.

He'd already decided on a likely alleyway in the town's main shopping area, and after checking to make sure no homeless cunts had bedded down there for the night, carried his burden down to the second industrial bin along, shoved back the lid, and dumped the bundle inside.

In the years he been doing this, he had only heard of one body ever being found. So long as you hauled a few larger pieces of rubbish over the bundle –or, in most cases, multiple bundles- the bins would be collected and emptied into the backs of the big waste lorries without anyone paying much close attention to what was actually in them... and off to landfill went the evidence.

The hammer went down a street drain.

He didn't go back to the flat. He'd paid up in advance, so that by the time the landlord came looking for his next payment, Letwin would have been long gone…and it was unlikely the flat's owner would investigate too deeply into any of the long dried brown stains left behind, not when a lick of paint would have the place ready for the next occupant.

Letwin was home by five o'clock the next evening, back to the loving bosom of his family, remembering to stop and pick up a couple of extra-large Toblerone bars at a motorway service station for his wife and his little girl, his usual apology for having to go away on business.

He didn't spare Carol another thought for months… not until December, in fact.

*****

She was outside Santa's grotto.

Letwin felt the bottom drop out of his guts, a plunging sensation that he had never felt before but which he quickly came to realise was sheer fucking terror.

Ivy had wanted to see Santa and so Letwin, the doting father and thoughtful husband, had suggested that they all go to the massive shopping and entertainment plaza just down the motorway for a day of Christmas present hunting and family time. Sophia could nip off and browse at leisure all morning whilst Letwin and Ivy went to see Santa, then on to watch a film before meeting mummy again for lunch.

There was a bit of a queue to see Santa, but that just gave Letwin and Ivy time to discuss what they should get mummy this year.

Santa was inside a cartoonish log cabin with fake snow on the bulls eye paned windows and candy cane pillars holding the roof up; children were allowed in one at a time to meet him, to tell him what they wanted, and receive a small present... for a discrete payment made by the parents.

The queue was being managed by an elf, who was keeping everyone entertained with jokes and small magic tricks.

It wasn't until they were three spaces from the front of the queue that Letwin recognised her.

If there had been any possibility of denial, it was killed before it had a chance to establish itself by the fact that not only was the tiny lady in the stripy elf costume the owner of a pair of silver, snow flake shaped eyes, but also had a face that was very finely threaded with fine white scars, like a China doll that had been smashed to pieces and then expertly reassembled.

Carol looked at him.

The snowflakes of her eyes glittered.

She grinned, and suddenly she was standing right in front of them with her hands on her hips.

She was half a head shorter than Ivy.

"Hello Ivy!" said the whore Letwin had killed, her voice as twinkly as the night he had smashed her face to shit with a claw hammer. "So, have you come to see my daddy?"

Ivy goggled, delighted.

"You know my name, how do you know my name?"

Carol winked at Letwin, but spoke to his little girl.

"Because I'm an elf, and we need to know who everyone is... and where we can find them! How else would you get your presents?"

This seemed logical, and having been resolved to the five-year-old's satisfaction allowed her to concentrate on the other curious thing the tiny lady had said.

Letwin said nothing. He couldn't.

He was trying not to lose his mind.

"Your daddy?" said Ivy. "Father Christmas is your daddy?"

"Weellll... that's what we call him," said Carol. She glanced behind her; they were at the front of the line. "Oh look Ivy, it's your turn! Go on, quick, quick! I know he's been looking forward to meeting you especially!"

And before Letwin could restrain her, the little girl was dashing for the open cabin door that was hung with a wreath and pillared by giant candy canes.

He took one hesitant step after her... but Carol placed her hand on his stomach which stopped him dead and suddenly it seemed there was no roaring shopping centre around them, no queue of fractious children and stressed out parents, piped in Christmas songs and smells of baking gingerbread.

There was just him and the elf and the open door to Santa's cabin.

"Just a minute, step you oh so lightly!" she said brightly, her eyes bright and sharp; snowflakes made from intersecting razor blades. "Auditions are always one on one!"

"I killed you," whispered Letwin.

Carol giggled. It sounded like bells ringing in a faraway land.

"You know when I told you about how we pay for Christmas?" asked Carol. "Didn't you wonder, even for a moment, if it wasn't just me, but the whole workshop... all of us? Christmas is expensive, you know. It's cheaper to have the toys made in export processing zones in third world countries where child labour laws don't exist. Toys for kids... made by kids!"

Letwin was staring at the open door through which his little girl had vanished.

"We made the change a few years back. So all year we would work the streets to make the money to pay for the toys..."

Auditions.

"But then you hired me because you thought I was a kid, and when I told daddy about that it gave him a great idea. We could make a lot more money if... well, if we have kids making the toys, why not get them to make the money to pay for them as well? It's like solving world hunger by eating the homeless!"

"Ivy!"

Suddenly he was moving, running for the open door, being followed by bright and twinkly laughter.

And when he got inside, and saw what the audition was, the first thing he felt was jealousy.

BEST SERVED COLD

THE THING that had been destined for dinner had escaped the confinement grid.

Oh, poo.

Calvin calculated.

He'd been asleep for his regular set of six REM cycles, which, in the worst case scenario, gave the thing nearly nine hours in which to have breached security and escaped the mansion.

Or worse; stayed inside the mansion and done who knew what? The dinner-thing had shown a disturbing level of intelligence, as well as a marked capacity for extreme violence.

Calvin's extended family had come for Christmas.

Calvin was rarely wrong, but his decision to let the dinner-thing continue to live until it could be butchered and cooked fresh on the big day was looking like a choice that may have gotten his entire bloodline wiped out.

The twelve-year-old hurried to the weapon case, armed himself, and prepared to hunt down Christmas dinner.

*****

Calvin Gooch, boy super-genius whose ideas and inventions had earned him a multi-billion fortune before he had turned double digits, believed there was no area of life that could not be improved if he simply turned his vast intellect upon it.

Such as the traditional British Xmas dinner of roast turkey.

Problem one; not everyone likes turkey.

Well, that had been solved already, right? The turducken was the answer, a dish whereby a chicken is stuffed inside a duck and that is then stuffed inside the turkey. Lots of different kind of bird meat, all there in one dish.

Calvin thought this culinary abomination was sadly lacking in vision, and thus had reinvented the turducken as the ostcassturduckenail.

Stuff a quail into the chicken, the chicken into the duck, the duck into the turkey, the turkey into a cassowary, and the whole fucking lot into an ostrich, the perfect meal for huge families like his own, all with fussy palates!

Calvin then cut out the middle man, the chef, by simply using his own modified CRISPR software to do some judicious DNA editing in his private zoo to create a creature which was much like those Russian nesting dolls, only using all the different bird species he planned to serve for Christmas day dinner.

Problem two; not everyone gets a drumstick.

And who doesn't love a drumstick?

Calvin calculated.

He fired up CRISPR again and mixed his ostcassturduckenail with his pet octopus, Cthulhu, and voila! The end result had eight titanic drumsticks the size of baseball bats to munch on!

*****

'Twas the night before Christmas, and all through the mansion, not a creature was stirring, not even uncle Hanson.

Or his wife, or their kids, Calvin's cousins.

He'd had the cy-servants make up the suite in the East wing for his holiday visitors. His uncle's brood were hyperactive and loud, especially their new-born, and he thought it best he put them at the far end of the building.

It was too quiet. The baby should have been squalling, or Cousin Martin should have still been up playing videogames.

Calvin calculated.

His Nanna's suite was closest.

He liked his Nanna, certainly more so than his father's brother and various genetic hangers-on. Especially Cousin Martin, who always beat Calvin at videogames.

Nanna would be saved first.

Calculations complete, he crept down the corridor. He was wearing night-vision goggles that rendered even the darkest rooms in shades of green. He didn't believe the diner-thing's eyesight was good in the gloom, and wanted to keep the advantage of having the lights off.

He carried a tranquiliser rifle. If at all possible, he still intended for the ostcassturduckenail to set the dinner table groaning under its juicy, stuffing packed weight.

The door to Nanna's suite was open.

There was slime on the handle.

He touched it with two fingers, brought it close to his nostrils. Calvin frowned, then popped his fingers in his mouth.

Not slime.

Gravy.

Oh, poo.

He'd done a little ad-lib gene editing with the dinner-thing to covert the octopus ink sacs into organs that made its own delicious sauce instead.

There was no doubt it had been here.

Calvin entered.

His Nanna's suite of rooms was decorated to look like a country cottage. Open fireplace with a hologram of a roaring fire, adjustable three speed rocking chair, the smell of baking bread and pastries pumped through vents in the ceiling.

The cy-servants had decorated it for the season in old-fashioned style, with handmade paper chains and pine cones sprayed silver and a big bowl of assorted nuts on the oak coffee table.

On the other side of the room, the door to Nanna's bedroom.

The door was ajar.

Stealthily, he crept up, and pushed it fully open with the muzzle of the gun.

His Nanna's body was tits-down naked on the bed, her arms and legs tied behind her.

Trussed up like a bird for the oven.

Her head was on the pillow.

Her mouth was held open with an onion.

There was something on the bedside table, something like a plastic bag with its bulging sides sagging over the edges of the table.

The dinner-thing wasn't in the room.

Long gone, its work done.

Calvin switched off his goggles and flicked on the light.

On the wall above the bed, carved onto the wall decorated with floral wallpaper, a word had been gouged by immense talons;

GIBLETS

It was a plastic bag on the bedside table, clear plastic that revealed the contents in all their gory glory.

Intestines, liver, stomach, kidneys, pancreas, her throat…

All of his Nanna's guts had been pulled out and neatly bundled up in a plastic bag… like giblets, the way you could buy your turkey at the shops with all of its guts in a bag stuffed up inside in case you wanted to cook them up for gravy.

Gravy…

Calvin snarled and dashed from the room, flipping down his night-vision goggles and selecting one of the modifications he had made for them. At the door to Nanna's suite he did an analysis scan on the gravy on the handle, and adjusted the goggles settings to track the chemical signature of the gloopy fluid.

The results were overlaid onto his field vision as purple traces on the monochrome rendering of the benighted mansion's corridor.

Long purple smears ran up the wall and across the ceiling... towards his parents wing of the mansion.

*****

The dinner-thing had restlessly prowled the perimeter of the containment area every hour of every day, occasionally lashing out at the electrified walls and screeching in bestial rage when it received a shock.

It hadn't been much to look at. Even with the most careful gene editing, you were never certain what you were going to get when the birthing-matrix ejected its organic load, but even still, the ostcassturduckenail was one ugly abomination.

It was a bit of a throw-back, in fact. Birds had descended from dinosaurs, and the dinner-thing definitely had a look of velociraptor to it... if those vicious killing machines had had eight immensely strong, boneless, talon hooked legs.

Calvin suspected it was the cassowary DNA that made the thing so violent, as those wild birds were vicious, but he hadn't suspected that the startling intelligence of an octopus had translated until he had idly asked, in a moment of what was for him uncharacteristic whimsy, with what kind of stuffing the ostcassturduckenail wished to be served?

The thing had answered him by scratching words onto the concrete floor of its enclosure with its talon tipped tentacles.

YOUR FUCKING BRAINS

*****

The parents of the *prodigy* son had an entire wing of the palatial building all to themselves.

Needless to say, from the earliest days when their son had displayed his truly astonishing abilities they had been happy to go along for the ride; Calvin's father had been a vending machine stockist who had quit his job not long after Calvin had made his first millions, aged eight years old, with an app that was now used by most of the world's population.

It was a strange relationship, where the child was the bread winner, but a child Calvin still was, and he still liked his dad to tuck him in at night and his mum to cook him fish fingers and spaghetti hoops for his tea… in return for which he paid his parents a generous amount of pocket money per month.

His parent's wing was the family home proper, even if Calvin only ate and slept there a few times a week, spending the majority of his time in his laboratories and office overseeing his rapidly growing business empire.

The door to the family home was ajar.

There was gravy slimed all over it.

Calvin entered.

His parents were in the first room, the living room that was decorated for a big traditional family Christmas.

His mum had been done up like his Nanna, legs and arms bent back and tied behind her so that she resembled a Xmas turkey destined for a date with the oven. She was on the floor, like a rug in front of the roaring fireplace, but instead of a bulging bag of her own guts sitting beside her as was the case with dear old Nanna, there was the corpse of Calvin's father, flat on his back with an erection and a frozen rictus grin.

He looked skinnier than he had only a few hours before.

Calvin commanded the lights on.

His mother was glistening, her entire body covered in thick, red blood that was not hers.

Even Calvin's remarkable mind couldn't quite work out what had happened, even with the word carved into the wall above the mantelpiece where hung the family stockings;

BASTING

Calvin called up the security camera feed for the room, setting it to rewind to the last time the motion sensors were triggered in the room.

A three dimensional holographic recording was projected onto the room itself, the images partially transparent, recording furniture overlapping the real furniture like a photon-film, and the moving figures of his soon-to-be-murdered parents and the dinner-thing was like watching a ghostly re-enactment of the horrific scene that had taken place only minutes earlier until eventually the projected images matched and overlaid the corpses.

The ostcassturduckenail had crawled across the ceiling, coming in from the bedroom where it had grabbed mum and dad, their bodies like puppets tangled in their own strings, though the strings were in fact tentacles dangling from the body of the genetic abomination slithering upside down across the room.

The dinner-thing broke mum's arms and legs and trussed them behind her. Calvin could have had sound, but seeing how wide his mother's mouth and eyes got as she screamed in agony convinced him not to turn it on.

When she could no longer move and as such no longer required a couple of tentacles to hold her, the dinner-thing was able to turn its full attention and all of its appendages onto dad.

Still gripping him around his chest and legs, one nimble sucker-lined arm darted between the man's legs and grabbed his cock…which it then proceeded to manipulate into an erection.

Though every room in the mansion had monitoring equipment in it, Calvin had respected the privacy of his family at all times, and had never even been tempted to watch his parents "doing it".

So this was wrong on every possible level.

His father's legs dangled inches above the ground, kicking feebly as the ostcassturduckenail vigorously jerked his erect cock.

Mum was still screeching and sobbing in soundless pain, and so at first she didn't react when dad ejaculated over her back.

Not the first time at least.

Nor the second, or third…

Calvin watched dumbfounded as the dinner-thing relentlessly tugged and throttled the meat tube which he himself had once shot out of as a spermatozoa, wanking and wanking his father to one joyless orgasm after another.

At some point it was no longer semen but blood shooting out of dad's cock to splatter his mum; the dinner-thing had wrapped tentacles around his stomach and torso like the bandages of an Egyptian mummy, and was squeezing him… this squeezing was what was forcing the gore to gush, basting Calvin's mother.

When it was done, after Calvin's father had had every drop of his blood squeezed out of his body via his penis, the ostcassturduckenail dropped the body and crawled across to the mantelpiece where three stockings hung. It used one claw to scratch the word BASTING into the wall, and then slithered from the room, leaving a slimy trail of gravy stains as it went.

The holographic recording ended.

Calvin gazed at his parent's corpses.

A single tear formed in the corner of his left eye, grew large enough that gravity found it and pulled it down his cheek.

He allowed himself this tiny trace of emotion, even though he knew it was irrational. The fact that he had his parent's DNA on file ready to clone them, as well as recent digitised brain wave scans that he could use to download their basic personalities into any new copies he might wish to make, meant feeling sad that they had been tortured to death was ridiculous.

But he was, when you got right down to it, still only a little boy, and he loved his mummy and daddy.

Having allowed himself this touch of irrationality, Calvin's thoughts returned to the business at hand.

There was only one place left for the dinner-thing to go.

*****

The guest wing was quiet... too quiet.

No baby cousin Matilda crying for a feed, no electronic explosions as cousin Martin played videogames late into the evening, no uncle Hanson snoring or aunt Jan telling him to shut the fuck up she was trying to get the baby back to sleep and Martin I told you to turn that off and go the fuck to bed or Santa won't bring you any fucking presents...

Calvin had always had a soft spot for his aunt's earthiness. He knew his extended family were, as his mum put it, "dog rough", but he had loved them for their frank manners and complete lack of refinement.

Family was family, after all. That was what made Xmas so special. That was why he wanted to make them the perfect Xmas dinner.

They were all certainly dead now though.

The rescue mission had become a matter of revenge.

Calvin entered the guest wing.

He had already guessed at what atrocity awaited him.

They were all in the main room.

Uncle Hanson had been a big man, and he was even bigger now that his wife, dear foul-mouthed aunt Jan, had been forced up his anus. Someone, his body hadn't burst asunder.

Aunt Jan's entire torso was stuffed up inside her husband, leaving only her hips showing. Cousin Martin had been forced feet-first back inside the vagina that had birthed him twelve years before...and the baby? To judge by the tiny legs sticking out of Martin's mouth, the dinner-thing must have crushed it into a thin tube by twisting it around and around like wringing a dishcloth before force feeding her to her brother.

The dinner-thing had turned the last of Calvin's family into a monstrous parody of a turducken, each stuffed inside the other.

As he stared at the gruesome scene, the hairs on the back of his neck began to prickle.

Slowly, Calvin turned around.

The ostcassturduckenail was lowering itself down from the ceiling like some insane spider. Atop its long ostrich neck, from between wattles and combs like obscene fungal growths, eyes blazed with hate and triumph.

It dropped the final few feet to the ground in a splatter of blood and gravy.

The giant genetic abomination hissed gently.

One tentacle-drumstick swung at the nearest wall and rapidly scratched a word with one sickle like talon.

PECKISH?

Calvin had abandoned the idea of trying to take it alive when he had first seen his nanny.

The gun he was carrying was a nifty weapon based on a pen that could write in four different colours, where all you had to do was give it a click to change between red and blue and black and green.

He'd applied the principle to armaments.

Why carry a machine gun and a flamethrower and a laser cannon and an acid sprayer when you could have just the one weapon that could switch between them all with a simple "click"?

He couldn't recall what it was set on.

It didn't fucking matter.

Calvin pulled the trigger.

A hail of lead exploded from the four-way muzzle.

The ostcassturduckenail elegantly weaved the bullets as it stalked forward like a spider.

Calvin twisted a dial and pulled the trigger again.

A geyser burst of sulphuric acid erupted.

The ostcassturduckenail jumped onto the ceiling, letting the corrosive fluid spray the ground where it had been, turning the carpet and floorboards into hissing muck.

And it kept coming.

Calvin twisted the dial again.

Pulled the trigger.

A searing beam of charged photons scorched across the ceiling, a blazing laser beam tracing back and forth as the dinner-thing dodged it. Calvin tried to follow its path, whipping the beam back and forth and even tracing figure-eights that caused massive chunks of plaster and masonry to crash to the ground.

The way the ostcassturduckenail moved was balletic, spinning and pirouetting out of the way of the searing white laser, its many claw tipped tentacles stabbing into the crumbling ceiling as it scurried spider-sure towards its target, eyes blazing in hateful triumph.

"Oh, poo," said Calvin, and turned the dial on his weapon to the final position.

The fireball that bloomed forth was mushroom shaped, its stalk the spewing jet of fuel with a cap ten feet in diameter.

The dinner-thing wasn't fast enough and was engulfed.

It screeched, a sound more dinosaur-like than bird, almost a genetic memory of its ancestors being roasted alive in the world-wide inferno triggered by the asteroid that wiped them out.

Calvin felt the skin on his face tighten and the hair on his head crisp as the intense heat washed back over him, but he kept his finger on the trigger and the jet of flame focussed on his experiment as it screamed and screamed.

It lost its grip and fell like a burning chandelier to the floor.

Eventually, the roar of the flamethrower was louder than the sounds of agony that the ostcassturduckenail was making, and Calvin released the trigger.

The flames died down.

The diner-thing bubbled and smoked and twitched.

And fell still.

Calvin, breathing hard, stood staring at it for a full minute, not trusting that it was dead. He was a boy genius, not a fool; there was no way he was going near it until he was certain...

Certain...

His nostrils flared.

He could smell... something... something... delicious.

Cautiously he approached the giant, terrible corpse.

It did not move.

Not even when he grabbed a baseball bat sized tentacle-leg, twisted it off with a meaty, gristly sound of tearing flesh, and held it up to his face.

Calvin breathed deeply.

It smelled just like Xmas.

He took a bite.

He chewed.

It was a bit dry.

Oh, poo.

Xmas dinner was ruined.

THE MEATBOY

ONCE UPON a time a little boy made a snowman in his back garden, and after placing a magic hat upon its head the snowman came to life and started screaming.

Think about it. It was made of snow. The first thing it saw when it looked around was piles of what it perceived as flesh and blood covering the ground.

The little boy had spent a good deal of time since his father had gone to work that morning making the snowman. He had rolled up two big balls for its body and its head. It had coal for eyes and a carrot for a nose.

The snowman continued to scream.

The little boy was quite alarmed at this turn of events. He had expected his creation to become his magical new best friend with whom he would go on all kinds of frosty-adventures, but instead it was standing in the middle of the garden screaming in terror as it stared all around with coal-lump eyes at a vision of Hell.

The little boy was only a little boy though, and was not able to make the imaginative leap to understanding what the snowman must be thinking and feeling.

He thought maybe he should get the fun started.

The little boy dug up a handful of fluffy white snow, tamped it into a round shape whilst being very careful that there were no stones in it because his father had said it was important you should NEVER throw snowballs with stones in them...and threw it at his new friend.

He giggled as the powdery projectile exploded right in the snowman's face.

The snowman stopped screaming.

The little boy giggled again, and began gathering up another couple of handfuls.

The snowman watched, in shock, in horror, as the child gouged more flesh and blood from the ground. It felt the remnants of the first salvo dripping down its face.

The little boy stood up and threw one, two, three more balls of ice crystals at the snowman.

One, two, three found their mark.

Splat, splat, splat.

The snowman stood very still as they hit him. Very still, except for one coal eye that began to twitch...

*****

The little boy's father came up the path home as quickly as he could, because there were long icy patches a bit like snail tracks all over the ground and he did not want to slip and hurt himself.

He was eager to spend the afternoon with his son. He had taken a half-day because snowfall was rare, and he had visions of forging a lifetime's happy memories with his boy.

They could go sledging on the big hill just down the road, and they could fall backwards into the drifts and make snow angels by swinging their arms and legs, and they could even build a...

His head full of daydreams, he was grinning like a little boy himself when something sailed through the air and hit him in the face with a splat.

He stopped dead in his tracks, stunned.

Then he grinned when he realised what was afoot.

A sneak attack!

Of course, the most fun you could have when the flakes fell and blanketed the world was to gather it up and make ammunition for a big...

The father wiped his face.

He did not wipe away snow.

The ball that had hit him had been a tight wad of torn muscle and streaky yellowish fat, all bound up in a wrapping of torn skin and hair.

There were teeth in it.

A memory of telling his little boy something important flashed through his mind.

Suddenly the father was not afraid of slipping on the icy patches, and he was sprinting as fast as he could around the side of the house towards the back garden where he had left his son playing earlier.

When he got there he saw the meatboy.

It was two big balls of shredded flesh and broken bones and twisted guts and organs, piled one atop the other. It had testicles for eyes and a penis for a nose.

And someone had put a magic hat on what it had for a head, so that it had magically come back to life.

It giggled, then threw another meatball at him.

LAST CHRISTMAS

THE NEWS reader announced the end of the world in a surprisingly chipper tone of voice.

This was not her fault.

The fault lay with the editor, who had assumed that the item about the Christmas star was a "puff" piece, the kind of item that came at the end of the news to end on a happy note after the usual grim list of disasters, atrocities, and gloom which made up a typical broadcast.

So the news reader's tone of voice was light and cheerful as she explained that universal extinction was scheduled in less than a fortnight.

"And finally, researchers analysing data from the Grinch-Krampus Deep Space telescope array have made a surprising discovery about the star that heralded the birth of Jesus Christ!

"As we all know, two thousand years ago a star was said to have appeared in the sky above Bethlehem on the day that the Messiah was born. It was this star, in fact, that was used by the Three Wise Men to navigate. The researchers have identified that this 'star' was in fact a super-nova, which is an explosion that happens when certain super-massive stars explode at the end of their lives"

"Fascinating stuff Ellen!" said the new-reader's co-host.

"Indeed, Tom! Furthermore, the Grinch-Krampus scientist's have estimated that the massive amounts of deadly gamma particles that were released by this super-nova two thousand years ago have been travelling through space all this time, and a wave of hard radiation is due to pass through our very own solar system in twelve days time..."

The news-reader's voice suddenly lost its chipper tone, and the colour drained out of her face. But she was a professional, and managed to get the last few words of the story out.

"...which will strip our planet of its atmosphere and kill all life on Earth, including the human race."

*****

Knowing that the world was coming to an end in less than a fortnight made people reassess their plans for the holiday season... though they didn't abandon their traditions all together.

*****

SUGINAMI, JAPAN

Junji Saitama reached for the bucket of KFC but then noticed that his hands were covered with blood, and so he instead picked up one of the small packets of pre-moistened napkins provided with the meal to clean his fingers first.

It was a topsy-turvy way of doing things, he observed. The cleansing napkins were supposed to be used after eating the greasy portions of chicken, not before.

But then, it had been a topsy-turvy sort of day.

Whilst he carefully wiped his hands clean of blood, he used the time to fully appreciate his own efforts.

Mr Takada the sales manager had assigned Saitama the task of organising the "office Christmas party". Mr Takada assigned all hard, worthless, or bizarre tasks to Saitama.

Saitama, as a low ranking salaryman at the Hi-Suda chromatography column manufacturing plant, had somehow attracted Mr Takada's ire from his very first day of work. He had no idea why.

This year, Mr Takada had wanted the company to celebrate Christmas the traditional "Western" way, and had tasked Saitama with arranging a suitable party at the office.

A Western Christmas office party... but Japanese. A fusion of traditions.

Mr Takada had spent a month visiting a manufacturing concern in the United Kingdom that year, and had grown enamoured with much of European culture. During his time there he had learned much about the regional sales of chromatography columns, as well as the local office culture... including the Christmas time celebration when co-workers would set aside an evening where they would all drink and eat together and all social boundaries were temporarily forgotten.

Saitama had meekly accepted the responsibility, heaped atop all the other responsibilities which were not technically part of his job.

The problem was, he had very little understanding of the Christmas holiday that Americans and Europeans made such a big deal about.

So he had set to research.

And grown confused.

Christmas, at its heart, revolved around two figures; the Jesus of the Christian religion, and the red robed figure of Santa Claus.

These two fictional men seemed to have nothing in common. Saitama was perplexed. How could this Western holiday revolve around both an ascetic saint, and an obese gift-giver?

Christmas was celebrated in Japan, of course, but in a much different way. It wasn't a proper holiday as such, but any excuse for a celebration was eagerly seized upon.

The only truly Japanese tradition was to buy and eat KFC. People ordered their Christmas dinner buckets days in advance. According to Saitama's research, the traditional Western dish of the day was a roast turkey or goose... so maybe things weren't so different.

Saitama had also researched the Western notion of the "office Christmas party". One thing he learned from translated blog posts was that very often at these events, thanks to alcohol, liaisons were often struck up between co-workers.

Which explained Mr Takada's interest.

...the dirty old man...

Saitama had begun to stress over organising a suitably Western-style office celebration of a puzzling mish-mash of notions. Christmas was supposedly the anniversary of the birth of Jesus... and yet a bearded man travelled the world in a single night and gave presents to other boys and girls. People were supposed to reflect on the holiness of the occasion, yet indulged in rampant materialism.

Or got drunk and forgot social protocol in the workplace with their colleagues.

Mr Takada asked for continual updates.

Saitama assured him all was going well with planning.

It was not.

And then the news about Doomsday broke.

Like people all over the world, Saitama took time to absorb the information. He reflected on how odd it was that the impending disaster was so closely linked to the advent of the event which had been stressing him for over a month.

Then, feeling the reality of his and everyone else's mortality upon him, he had gone quietly and purposefully insane.

He had gone to see his boss at home.

It was Mr Takada's wife who had answered the door.

Looking at Mrs Takada, Saitama understood why his boss would like the opportunity to break the usually strict social boundaries between himself and the other employees of Hi-Suda Chromatography... or at least, the female ones, plied with alcohol.

Or, "Christmas cheer."

Saitama introduced himself, apologised deeply for the intrusion, and then shot her in the face with the nail gun he was carrying.

The nails burst her eyes and blasted her teeth out of her mouth.

Mr Takada had foolishly come to find out what the screaming was about, and found his put-upon employee waiting for him.

Saitama's boss took a high-pressure nail in the belly and two in the right knee, splitting his knee-cap, before he agreed to do what Saitama asked of him.

The request was to put on a costume.

Mr Takada's wife had screamed for help and clawed at what used to be her eyes whilst her husband had painfully removed his clothes and "donned the gay apparel" his underling had brought.

Then, when Mr Takada was dressed in the red suit with white trimmings and was wearing the great big false beard of snowy curls, Saitama had nailed his hands to the wall.

Then his testicles.

Mr Takada had screamed and ranted and thrashed his head around, which caused the floppy pointed hat to keep falling off.

So Saitama had used the gun to nail it to his skull.

His decorating done, he found a nearby KFC on his phone that was open despite so many people no longer showing up for work since Doomsday was announced.

He ordered in.

With Santa Claus crucified, Junji Saitama happily munched fried chicken and congratulated himself on a perfect fusion of East and West Christmas traditions.

*****

TARRAGONA, SPAIN

For the past year it seemed that Zoraida Dali's entire world had revolved around shit.

She worked as a cleaner in an office building. Every floor had four different bathrooms shared by the various businesses that worked in the building. From six until midnight she cleaned toilets. Then when she arrived home she had cloth nappies to attend to.

Zoraida did not have a child, but elderly and incontinent parents. The nappies were theirs.

Her brothers and sister had agreed that papa and mama needed fulltime care, and that Zoraida, being the youngest and unmarried, should move back to the family home to take care of them.

This agreement had been made at the big Christmas feast almost exactly one year ago. At the big kitchen table groaning under a huge pot of *escudella i carn d'olla* Zoraida had been blindsided; evidently her siblings had decided the issue before hand and kept quiet so that she had no chance to argue for an alternative.

So she had moved home, leaving nursing college. Her family assured her it was just as well; she had only decided to become a nurse when it was clear she was not smart enough to be a doctor.

And if she wanted so badly to be a nurse, what excellent practice, to care for her parents!

To feed them. To clean them. To organise their medication.

So this was her life now. She cleaned up the shit of complete strangers for a living, and cleaned up the shit of her own parents whilst at home.

Her parents were on different sets of medication for age related ailments which gave them different bowel movements. Mama's were thin and orange, more liquid than solid, whilst papa's were almost black, hard, and scaly.

At the office building each evening it was pot luck what nightmares might have been left behind in the forty odd toilets she was expected to scrub. Crusts around the rim, carefully coiled turds in the water, or shy little turtle heads peeking out from around the u-bend.

Shit all day, shit all evening.

Zoraida was exhausted, mentally and physically. She was only able to get through the days and weeks and months of shit and more shit by telling herself that her parents would not be around forever, and that her cleaning job was only temporary as she worked towards an online diploma in pharmacy dispensing.

Then Christmas time had come looming and Zoraida learned that she would also be responsible for having the family around for the big day.

After all, it was the family home. It was tradition.

Her siblings had pointed out that mama and papa did not have many more Christmases ahead of them. How could she be so selfish as to deny them the big family get together they had known all their lives!

Zoraida had relented, and just yesterday had retrieved the decorations from the attic.

Chief amongst these, of course, was the Nativity figurines... and dear old Tio.

Zoraida had almost finished setting up the Nativity when the news on the radio had confirmed the findings of the Grinch-Krampus telescope team.

This was the very last Christmas.

She had been putting out the figurines that were older than her, part of a set which had been handed down from her great-great-grandparents – the wise men, Mary, Joseph, the Saviour, and the attendant animals- when she had stopped to listen to the report.

When the news had finished she had switched off the radio.

The world was going to end.

A thought floated freely in her mind, like a stubborn turd circling in an overflowing toilet bowl;

My parents did not need to kill my dreams, for they were dead anyway.I simplydid not know it... no-one did.

She had looked at the figurine in her hand. She was holding the *Caganer*.

Zoraida had blinked at it, stunned.

In the Catalan region of Spain, nativity scenes have a strange additional character known as the *Caganer*. This figure was of a boy wearing a *barretina*, the traditional slouch cap of Catalonia, with his trousers pulled down, defecating.

The meaning of such a profane idol added to the holy diorama depicting the birth of Jesus was obscure, but Zoraida's father had once explained it to her.

"God became human," he'd said one Christmas long ago, when the future was still hopeful and the young girl had dreams of becoming a doctor. Around her neck was a toy stethoscope, a present she had asked for. "That is the single most important fact of the Incarnation. Man is part spirit and part animal. God the spirit became animal. And what is more animal, more distant from divinity, than the fact of shitting?"

Zoraida was a fiercely bright child, and had asked if that was why Tio appeared by the fireplace every Christmas was well?

Her father allowed that it could be so.

Zoraida, in the grip of memory as she processed the news that the human race was doomed, had glanced towards the fireplace.

Tio de Nadal was there, as he was every year.

The thing was a wooden log with a smiling face painted on one end, half draped with a cloth. During the Christmas period, each night, her brothers and her sister and Zoraida herself had been tasked with "feeding" Tio a nut or a piece of candy... and every dawn Tio would have grown a little more. Then, on Christmas morning, when Tio would be the size of the biggest log on the fire having been fed by the children each evening... then they would attack him!

Another Catalan tradition, every household had a *Tio de Nadal*. The trick was simple, there were a set of Tio's ranging from tiny to full size, and each night parents would replace the previous log with a slightly larger one so that it appeared that he was growing.

On Christmas morning everyone would be given a stick to beat Tio with whilst singing;

> *Shit, log, shit!*
> *Almonds and nougats!*
> *Do not shit herrings*
> *(They are too salty)*
> *Shit nougats*
> *(Which are better)*
> *Shit, log, shit!*
> *Almonds and nougats,*
> *And if you don't want to shit...*
> *I will give you a smack!*

And then the cloth that half covered him would be pulled away to reveal a pile of candies and nuts which he had defecated for the children.

Zoraida felt the ghost of a smile on her face as she gazed at the "shitting log", remembering beating him with her siblings as a child.

And then she frowned, looking at the *Caganer* she still held.

Shit.

Everything... was...

Shit.

Zoraida Dali felt a great calm wash over her.

She had finished setting out the decorations, attended to her parent's needs of dinner and nappy changing, and had headed out to her cleaning job.

She was one of only two staff who turned up that evening. Zoraida supposed it was because people were upset that the dirty, dreary world was soon to come to a close.

It made what she planned to do a lot easier.

She left long before midnight.

When she arrived home, her father was still awake. Mama was snoring gently in the bed next to him.

He greeted her with a confused smile. Shouldn't she still be at work?

Zoraida had set the cooler on his lap. It was the small kind you would take on picnics.

It had curious stains around the lid.

"Papa," Zoraida had said, standing over the bed with her hands behind her back. "It would seem that this is to be our last Christmas together. You and mama have such trouble getting about these days, so I thought I would bring one of our traditions to you."

"What is this, child?" her father had asked. His eyes were milky with cataracts, but his nose was as keen as ever. "Such a stink!"

Zoraida's hands came out from around her back.

In one she held a stethoscope.

In the other, a spoon.

She pressed the spoon into one of her father's hands, and then flipped the lid of the cooler open.

Tio was floating on the top of the semi-solid contents.

"I have brought some work home with me," said Zoraida. "Eat up, papa!"

She lashed her father's bare chest with the stethoscope, whipping him with the metal earpieces so fiercely that they drew blood.

He cried out.

And as if she were carrying the tune, Zoraida began to sing about almonds and nougats, whipping her father over and over and over again until he finally began to feed.

*****

EGILSSTADIR, ICELAND

Gunnar Hreinson had done a lot of reading since his father shot the television and started drinking himself unconscious each day.

Gunnar was a good reader, but over the past few days he had encountered words which were entirely new to him, like *Ragnarok*, *Gotterdammerung*, *Apocalypse*, and *Armageddon*.

As far as the seven year old understood it, they all meant the same thing.

But he wasn't sure what it was.

He tried asking his father.

Pabbi would know... but pabbi was acting strangely.

Gunnar's father Hrein had been drinking *brennivin* steadily since the announcement of the end of the world. Whilst he had managed to make meals for Gunnar, he had not been going to work at the aluminium smelting plant, or taking his son to school, only leaving their sky-blue corrugated iron home to go to the local Vinbuoin to stock up on alcohol. But in his way he had been trying to be a good father; as he had sat at the kitchen table drinking "black death" until he blacked-out each day he had been trying to decide how to end his and his son's lives.

The gun was the obvious choice.

But could he do it? Could he shoot his only son, even to spare him from the nightmare that was coming?

After the announcement, a few of the television channels that had continued to operate had brought in scientific men and women to explain what was to be expected when the hard radiation hit the earth.

The air would boil. The oceans would boil. Animals and plants and people would *boil*.

Hrein had been waiting for someone to say it was all a joke.

But when nobody did, he went to his gun closet, selected his favourite hunting rifle, and blasted the television.

His boy must not hear any talk of *boiling*.

But now Gunnar had come to him asking him the meaning of some strange foreign words.

The boy's face was serious.

He looked so much like his mother.

Hrein asked Gunnar where he had heard such gobbledygook.

Gunnar said he had been online.

Hrein groaned. He had forgotten about the laptop, and how technologically literate his child was.

I should have shot the computer as well.

Gunnar explained.

He only really read Icelandic, but very little content on the net was written in it, so he had been trying to run news articles through a translator, but they had stumbled over the big, weird words.

His question was in three parts; what was "Armageddon", and was it more important than Christmas, and was it why the Yule Lads had not come to visit so far this Christmas?

Hrein had blinked at his son. The seven year old had made his queries all in one long, multi-segmented rush, and Hrein was drinking hard liquor without even a spoonful of *skyr* in his belly to soak it up.

Yes, it was Christmas wasn't it?

And Armageddon.

It was... the star that announced the birth of Jesus... cosmic radiation, mega-death...

If only Erla were here to help explain.

The Yule Lads had not been to visit.

Gunnar was only worried about this "Armageddon" because it was interfering with

Christmas. It meant the Yule Lads had not been to visit!

Hrein smiled to himself.

The thirteen children of the giantess Gryla, who came to town for the thirteen nights leading up to Christmas day, to play pranks and make mischief and leave gifts in the shoes of good boys and girls. Could he name them all? Yes, even as drunk as he was, Hrein could name all thirteen of the monstrous but merry Yule Lads;

Sheepcote Clod, Gully Gawk, Stubby, Spoon-Licker, Pot-Scraper, Bowl-Licker, Door-Slammer, Skyr-Gobbler, Sausage-Swiper, Window-Peeper, Doorway-Sniffer, Meat-Hook... and Candle-Stealer!

He recalled his own childhood, putting his shoes on the windowsill each evening in the hope that whichever Yule Lad dropped by the house that night would leave him a small gift, rather than a potato, which was what bad girls and boys received.

"Pabbi?"

Gunnar's voice broke his drunken reverie.

"Pabbi? Will they come?"

"Hmm?"

"The Yule Lads. It's been three days and I don't think they've been, because I've had nothing in my shoes. Are they coming? Will they be here before Armageddon?"

Hrein Olafurson had been drinking the caraway flavoured liquor called brennivin for hours, and until his son's innocent, worried question he had been heading towards drunken oblivion.

He had yet to reach the point where he was able to use the rifle.

Boiling.

The quiet pleading in Gunnar's voice as he stumbled over a word that simply meant "doom" sobered him instantly.

It was Christmas.

A time of light and laughter in the grim dark and cold of mid-Winter. A time of wonder, and love.

Yet the Yule Lads hadn't even come.

What would Erla have thought?

An idea entered his head, the kind only men deep inside of alcohol can get; simple, and brilliant, and unthinkable outside the logic of hard liquor.

Hrein put the bottle down and gripped his son's shoulder.

"The Yule Lads have not come to visit my boy?" he said, his eyes focussing and unfocussing as he spoke. "Those scoundrels! Those curs! Those rotten fuckers! Well! If the Yule Lads will not come to us, Gunnar, then I say we should go to them!"

Gunnar looked puzzled and a little scared.

"What do you mean pabbi?" he asked.

Hrein pushed himself away from the table and stood unsteadily, placing his hands on his hips.

"These Yule Lads, they live with their mamma Gryla and their step-father Leppluoi in a cave in the mountains, right? Well, it so happens that I know exactly which cave!"

Gunnar looked astonished.

"You know where they live?" he asked in awe.

"Of course I do!" said Hrein. "Quickly, Gunnar, put on your coat and your mittens and your boots, I think we should pay a visit on these Lads and see what they have to say for themselves! Did they not come to visit my boy these past few nights? Why, I'll knock their heads together! I'll skin their ears! I'll make them eat dung! I'll... I'll..."

"Bash their butts!" cried Gunnar, laughing.

"That's right! We'll bash their butts!"

"Where is their cave, pabbi?" Gunnar asked.

His father waved a hand

"Not far, not far," he said. "Now quick, quick Gunnar, go and dress yourself warmly! We've heads to knock together, and butts to bash!"

And Gunnar, believing his father, ran off.

Hrein watched his son dash for the little room where they stored the thick outer garments needed for the Icelandic winters.

He would make them a flask each of hot cloudberry juice, and wrap some *hangikjot* and *laufabrauo* bread to eat, and they would make an adventure of it.

Yes! They could have themselves a fine time. A wonderful Christmas to remember for the rest of their lives!

And for a moment he lived inside the fantasy.

It was just long enough.

Hrein started to cry.

When Gunnar came running back into the kitchen dressed for festive fun, his face was bright and open, grinning, and his father shot him in the head.

*****

Carnage. Destruction. Riots. Rape. Murder.

Forget the partridge in the pear tree.

Twelve days in which humanity lost hope, then lost its mind. Every wicked thought squashed by the constraints of the social contract surfaced. Itchy trigger fingers got scratched. Scores were settled. Dark and shameful fantasies hitherto repressed were acted upon.

A surprising number of the population came out as cannibals.

The blood dimmed tide was loosed. Cities burned. Civilisation died screaming.

Then twelfth night arrived.

For the first time in history, the world was quiet as everyone looked skywards.

When it started, it looked like the aurora borealis, only it was the entire sky, everywhere.

It was beautiful.

And when it was over there was finally, forever, peace on Earth.

www.ingramcontent.com/pod-product-compliance
Lightning Source LLC
Chambersburg PA
CBHW022053170626
46808CB00003B/1458